The *Supernatural* Quiz Book Season 6

500 questions and answers on *Supernatural* Season 6

Light Bulb Quizzes

Written by fans, for fans

Unofficial

Published by Light Bulb Quizzes

ISBN 978-0-9932030-5-3

Edited by
Kim Kimber
www.kimkimber.co.uk

Cover artwork by
White Tree Fine Art
www.facebook.com/whitetreefineart
www.whitetreefineart.co.uk

All of the questions in this quiz book are based on the DVD release of *Supernatural* Season 6, produced by Warner Home Video and the soundtrack and other details may sometimes vary from that of other versions.

This book is unofficial and unauthorised. All of the questions have been researched and compiled by Light Bulb Quizzes who have done their best to ensure that all information is correct. However, if any sharp-eyed *Supernatural* fans notice an error, please contact us so that it can be rectified.

For all fans of
Supernatural

Contents

Introduction

Following on from our previous books, *The Supernatural Quiz Book Season 6* continues our nostalgic look at past seasons of the cult American TV series, *Supernatural.*

At the start of Season 6, Dean (Jensen Ackles) is attempting to live a normal life, away from hunting, with Lisa Braeden (Cindy Sampson) and Ben (Nicholas Elia) but can't quite seem to let go of his past completely. When his brother, Sam, (Jared Padalecki) turns up having been mysteriously freed from Lucifer's cage, Dean finds himself caught between his old life and new family. As it becomes apparent that Sam is far from his usual empathetic self and angel Castiel (Misha Collins) is being increasingly secretive and untrustworthy, Dean finds himself being drawn back into life as a hunter with heart-breaking consequences for Lisa and Ben.

Written and produced by members of the fandom, for other fans to enjoy, this latest quiz book by Light Bulb Quizzes provides another chance to revisit past seasons and episodes and remember the many unforgettable moments that have made *Supernatural* such a popular and enduring series.

Our aim, as always, is to entertain and inform and our books cover all aspects of *Supernatural* from the cast, monsters and storylines through to lesser known facts and trivia.

Together, our books form a complete overview of the series and we hope that you will join us we continue to look back fondly at the road so far…

Light Bulb Quizzes

Written by fans, for fans

'You get to work with a partner. You get to help people. You have no idea what's in some people's walls.'

~ Dean Winchester

Questions

Episode 1 – Exile on Main St.

1. What does Dean keep under the bed in his new life with Lisa and Ben?

2. At the bar, how does Dean describe his past work to his neighbour, Sid?

3. What is underneath Dean's doormat?

4. What three things does Dean notice that, as a hunter, make him suspicious?

5. What old adversary does Dean see in his garage?

6. What has happened to Dean and who saves him?

7. How does Dean's rescuer prove that he is human?

8. How long has Sam been back and who are his new hunting pals?

9. Where does Dean take Lisa and Ben for protection?

10. Why did Bobby not tell Dean that his brother was alive?

11. What kind of monster is after Dean and Sam and why?

12. Which one of the cousins is killed when the above goes after Dean's neighbours – Christian, Mark or Johnny Campbell?

13. What do Samuel and the other cousins do with the female monster?

14. True or false: Dean returns to hunting with Sam and their relatives?

15. What does Dean offer to give Sam at the end of the episode?

Episode 2 – Two and a Half Men

16. What is being taken from people by the monster?

17. Why does Dean shout at Ben?

18. What do all the victims have in common?

19. What does Sam find in the house?

20. What does Dean teach Lisa before going to help Sam?

21. What tries to take the baby from the supermarket?

22. What does Dean give the baby to stop it from crying?

23. What is Dean's theory about the child?

24. What happens to the baby's 'real' father?

25. Where do Dean and Sam take the baby to keep it safe?

26. A shapeshifter appears in whose form in order to take custody of the baby – Dean, Lisa or Samuel Campbell?

27. What is special about this shapeshifter?

28. Why do Dean and Samuel think this might be?

29. Which one of the Campbell cousins is killed in the fight?

30. What do Dean and Lisa decide at the end of the episode?

Season 6 Episode Titles

Can you name the Season 6 episode titles from the clues?

31. The title of a 1949 film noir written by Graham Greene and starring Orson Welles.

32. This episode shares its title with a 1984 song by American singer, Madonna.

33. A novella by Rudyard Kipling, later made into a 1975 movie directed by John Huston and starring British actors Sean Connery and Michael Caine.

34. Title of the infamous autobiography by Christina Crawford, Joan Crawford's adopted daughter, later made into a movie starring Faye Dunaway.

35. This episode shares its title with a well-known American sitcom that aired 2013-15, originally starring Charlie Sheen.

36. Reference to a quote from J.M. Barrie's timeless play *Peter Pan*.

37. The title of 1974 movie written and directed by *Silence of the Lambs* (1991) director Jonathan Demme.

38. This episode title references a famous novel, first published in 1939, by crime writer Agatha Christie.

39. Well-known quote by Colonel Nathan Jessup (Jack Nicholson) from the 1992 movie *A Few Good Men*.

40. This episode references a sequence in the 1974 movie *Blazing Saddles,* directed by Mel Brooks.

41. A themed land at the Walt Disney World resorts depicting the Wild West.

42. The title of a 1989 animated movie featuring the voice of Burt Reynolds.

43. The title of a song by Celine Dion featured in the 1997 movie *Titanic*.

44. A 1934 suspense movie directed by Alfred Hitchcock, remade in 1956 starring James Stewart and Doris Day.

45. The episode shares its title with a 1990s sitcom featuring the Winslow family and their annoying nerdy neighbour, Steve Urkel.

Episode 3 – The Third Man

46. Who is Dean dreaming about at the beginning of the episode?

47. What does Dean tell Ben he is a professional at?

48. What is strange about Christopher Burch according to Ed?

49. Who does Dean pray to for help?

50. What does the above tell Sam that he and Dean share?

51. What weapon is being used to cause plague symptoms?

52. What skills does Castiel say are rusty?

53. Who has the Staff of Moses?

54. True or false: The above gave his soul to a demon in exchange for the staff?

55. Who gave Aaron the Staff?

56. What has happened to the Staff, has it been – destroyed, cut into pieces or given to Raphael?

57. How does Castiel find out the whereabouts of the Staff?

58. Who wants to take over heaven?

59. What does Balthazar do to Raphael's vessel?

60. What does Sam admit to Dean?

Episode 4 – Weekend at Bobby's

61. Who directed this episode?

62. What does Bobby want from Crowley?

63. The demon that Bobby is torturing tells him what about Crowley?

64. What do the demons call Crowley behind his back?

65. What does Bobby's neighbour, Marcy, bring round for him?

66. What is Crowley's human name?

67. Who turns up at Bobby's house asking for help – Dean and Sam, Sheriff Jody Mills or Rufus Turner?

68. Who does the resurrected lamia target as her next victim?

69. How does Bobby dispose of the above monster?

70. How does Rufus hide Crowley's son's ring?

71. How does Bobby describe Dean and Sam?

72. Why did Crowley sell his soul?

73. Who releases Rufus from police custody?

74. Who flies to Scotland and why?

75. True or false: Crowley agrees to release Bobby from his contract?

Season 6 Quotes

Who says the following during Supernatural Season 6?

76. 'Keep talking dirty. Makes my meatsuit all dewy.'

77. 'What do you think the soul is? Some pie you can slice? The soul can be bludgeoned, tortured, but never broken. Not even by me.'

78. 'Yeah, well, the guy that basically just saved the world shows up at your door, you expect him to have a couple of issues.'

79. 'Am I the only game piece on the board who doesn't underestimate those denim-wrapped nightmares?'

80. 'You wanted the real me. This is it. I don't care about them. I don't even really care about you.'

81. 'The footsteps I'm following, they're yours. What you did, stopping the big plan, the prize fight. You did more than rebel. You tore up the whole script and burned the pages for all of us. It's a new era. No rules, no destiny. Just utter and complete freedom.'

82. 'You're nothing but ghosts with an ego.'

83. 'I said we've had this conversation already. And you could blabber all day... and it wouldn't change a thing... I will never forgive you for what happened. You got that? Never.'

84. 'Of course. Your problems always come first. I'll be in touch.'

85. 'When your kind first huddled around the fire, I was the thing in the dark. Now you think you can hurt me?'

86.   'Cheer up, mate, we just saved the sodding world together. Me, I've been celebrating.'

87.   'Well, that's great. Because without your power, you're basically just a baby in a trenchcoat.'

88.   'Your father made you and then abandoned you, so you pray…A mother would never abandon her children like He did.'

89.   'Your chocolate's been in my peanut butter for far too long.'

90.   'When you've done this job as long as I have, a giant from the future with some magic brick doesn't exactly give you the vapours.'

Episode 5 – Live Free or Twihard

91. What is the name of the club in the first scene – The White Fang, The Red Heart or The Black Rose?

92. What is the name of the latest female victim?

93. What is the password for the above girl's laptop?

94. What famous book and film series is being referenced?

95. What is the name of the vampire that catches Kristen?

96. How many girls have disappeared?

97. The victim's room is a shrine to what kind of monster?

98. What happens to Dean?

99. Who watches this happen?

100. Who does Dean visit after he is 'turned'?

101. From whom do Dean and Sam get the cure?

102. In order to be turned back to a normal human state what must Dean *not* do?

103. What is the ingredient Dean must get from the vampires' nest for the cure?

104. Where do the vampires' orders come from?

105. What is the alpha vampire trying to do?

Episode 6 – You Can't Handle the Truth

106. What does the little girl want to do to her mother?

107. What does Bobby tell Dean about Sam?

108. How does Sam know the suicide victim's sister was lying?

109. What does the dentist do to the patient after he tells the truth?

110. What do the two suicide victims have in common?

111. What does Dean think is making everyone tell the truth?

112. What is the real reason everyone is telling the truth?

113. What happens to the suicide victims' bodies?

114. How does the 'curse' fall on Dean?

115. What two things does Bobby confess to Dean?

116. How does Lisa describe Dean and Sam's relationship?

117. Who is the truth god posing as?

118. What is Sam able to do to the god of truth?

119. What does Sam admit to Dean?

120. True or false: Dean's response is to punch his brother in the face?

Season 6 Soundtrack

121. In episode 1 'Exile on Main St.' what song plays during the opening montage of Dean's life away from hunting?

122. What Kenny Rogers song features in episode 4 'Weekend at Bobby's'?

123. In what scene in episode 21 'Let It Bleed' does 'Smiling Faces Sometimes' by The Undisputed Truth play?

124. In episode 9 'Clap Your Hands if You Believe' what music is playing when Dean is confronted by the fairy?

125. How many songs by Federale, a band that plays western music, are featured in episode 18 'Frontierland' – one, two or three?

126. In which Season 6 episode does 'One Way or Another' by American band Blondie feature?

127. In episode 20 'The Man Who Would Be King' what song plays in Crowley's torture chamber?

128. What song by Kansas does Dean quote to the man who dies of a heart attack in episode 11 'Appointment in Samarra'?

129. Which famous waltz composed by Johann Strauss features in episode 20 'The Man Who Would Be King'?

130. What song by Jethro Tull features in episode 12 'Like a Virgin'?

131. What song by Deep Purple features in episode 2 'Two and a Half Men'?

132. What episode features 'Love Hurts' by Nazareth?

133. What song is being played in the bar at the beginning of episode 19 'Mommy Dearest'?

134. What Rolling Stone song is playing in the background in the cage in episode 22 'The Man Who Knew Too Much'?

135. How many episodes of *Supernatural* Season 6 do not feature a soundtrack?

Episode 7 – Family Matters

136. What can Sam no longer do since he got back from hell?

137. What does Castiel discover about Sam?

138. How tall does Castiel say his true form was?

139. Who else was resurrected one year ago?

140. Does the above have a soul?

141. What have Sam and his granddad, Samuel, been doing with the monsters including the alpha?

142. What has Samuel put on the outside of the warehouse as a vampire repellent – sigils, dead man's blood or garlic?

143. What does Samuel do to the alpha vampire?

144. Who is the alpha?

145. Where do vampires (like all monsters) go when they die?

146. What is Christian?

147. Who is Samuel being controlled by?

148. True or false: the above pulled Sam and Samuel out of hell?

149. What TV programme did Crowley reference with regards to his relationship with the Winchesters and Samuel?

150. What does Crowley use as a bargaining chip with Dean and Sam?

Episode 8 – All Dogs Go To Heaven

151. What happens to the man at the beginning of this episode?

152. Who has a job for Dean and Sam?

153. What does the above do to Sam?

154. What deal does Crowley propose to Dean?

155. Why does Dean think they are not hunting a werewolf?

156. What does Sam tell Dean?

157. What happens to the dock worker?

158. What relation are the victims to Cal?

159. What happens to Cal after Dean and Sam stop watching him that night?

160. What happens to the creature?

161. Who does Sam suspect?

162. What does Sam see when he is keeping an eye on Mandy's house?

163. What happens to Lucky?

164. What is the creature the boys are hunting?

165. What does Sam admit to Dean?

166. How do you distinguish between a djinn and a human?

167. We have seen the djinn before, how many episodes have the djinn appeared in from their first appearance in Season 2 to Season 6 – two, three or four?

168. What is the difference between a normal and an alpha shapeshifter?

169. What is an alpha shapeshifter's weakness?

170. What is an alpha vampire?

171. Who is Veritas?

172. What is her power?

173. What can kill a skinwalker?

174. Who can see fairies?

175. What happens if you spill sugar or salt in front of them?

176. How do you kill a lamia?

177. What does lamia mean in Greek?

178. What creature do you kill with a blade made out of dragon's blood?

179. What can the venomous bite of an arachne do?

180. What creature enters the body through the ear and leaves behind black goo?

Episode 9 – Clap Your Hands If You Believe…

181. Where are the young couple at the beginning of the episode?

182. What famous American science fiction drama is referenced in the opening sequence??

183. What do people believe is behind the disappearances?

184. What is actually taking people?

185. Dean is taking the role of what for Sam?

186. Can you name the first victim?

187. Where does Dean find Sam when he escapes from the fairies?

188. What is unusual about the above encounter?

189. What does Dean do to the ball of light; his attacker?

190. Who do the fairies target and abduct?

191. How do you get a fairy's attention?

192. Why does Mr Brennan make a deal with a leprechaun?

193. Why does Dean get arrested?

194. What effect does cream have on fairies?

195. How does Sam stop the leprechaun?

Episode 10 – Caged Heat

196. Who is Crowley seemingly beating up at the beginning of this episode?

197. What has Crowley caught?

198. What is Crowley's knife made out of?

199. Who catches Dean and Sam?

200. What does Sam propose to their above capturer?

201. Sam tricks Castiel by telling him the plot of which action movie?

202. What is Castiel watching on TV that surprises Dean?

203. Why doesn't Castiel think Sam should have his soul back?

204. What is Crowley holding over Samuel?

205. What is guarding Crowley's torture chamber – demons, hellhounds or vampires?

206. How does Samuel get rid of Castiel?

207. True or false: Samuel betrays Dean and Sam to Crowley?

208. Dean is going to be dinner, for what kind of monsters?

209. How do Dean and Sam catch Crowley?

210. What does Castiel do to Crowley?

Jensen Ackles (Dean Winchester)

211. What name were Jensen's parents originally going to call him?

212. Why did they change their minds?

213. What star/zodiac sign is Jensen – Aquarius, Pisces or Aries?

214. How tall is Jensen?

215. Which actress and model did Jensen marry in November 2009?

216. True or false: Jensen is a keen golfer?

217. For what animated video-film did Jensen provide the voice of Jason Todd/Red Hood in 2010?

218. What fictional superhero has Jensen said that he would love to play?

219. What theme links Jensen's roles in *Days of Our Lives*, the movie *Devour* and *Supernatural*?

220. In 2010, Jensen was nominated for an *Entertainment Weekly* Award for Best Actor in a Drama Series, did he win?

221. In 2011, Jensen won a *TV Guide* Award for his role as Dean Winchester in *Supernatural,* in what category?

222. Jensen only voiced Dean Winchester in *Supernatural: The Anime Series* in 2011, for two episodes, can you name them?

223. What character does Jensen voice in the 2010 video game Tron: Evolution?

224. For what role on *Supernatural* did Jensen originally audition?

225. What episode of *Supernatural* Season 6 did Jensen direct?

Episode 11 – Appointment in Samarra

226. What is the name of the doctor Dean visits?

227. Where is he based?

228. How many minutes does Dean have – one, three or five?

229. Who or what is Dean looking for?

230. How can the above help Sam?

231. What is Death's condition?

232. Can you name the reaper helping Dean?

233. What angel does Sam summon?

234. As part of the above angel's deal, who does Sam need to kill?

235. How does Sam's intended victim escape?

236. Why does Dean take off Death's ring?

237. Who does Dean refuse to kill?

238. Who is sitting at Bobby's table eating?

239. What does Death bring Dean for dinner?

240. True or false: Death decides to return Sam's soul even though Dean loses their wager?

Episode 12 – Like a Virgin

241. What flies past the plane window?

242. What does Castiel say Sam's soul feels like?

243. What is the last thing Sam remembers?

244. What does Dean take from the girl's room?

245. What do the victims have in common?

246. What website does Sam's research lead him to?

247. Who does Bobby send Dean to see?

248. What sword does the doctor have?

249. What does Dean use to try and get the sword out of the stone?

250. True or false: Bobby accidentally reveals to Sam that he was raised from hell without his soul and has only just got it back?

251. Where is the dragon hiding – in caves, in a forest or in the sewers?

252. Apart from female victims, what else does the dragon take?

253. What is the ancient book they find made of?

254. What are the virgins going to be used for?

255. Who is let out of Purgatory at the end of the episode?

Jared Padalecki (Sam Winchester)

256. Prior to *Supernatural* Jared played another character called Sam, in what TV movie?

257. In what TV series did Jared famously play a character named Dean?

258. What star/zodiac sign is Jared – Gemini, Cancer or Leo?

259. How tall is Jared?

260. Which *Supernatural* actress did Jared marry in February 2010?

261. Where did the wedding take place?

262. True or false: Jared is not superstitious in real life?

263. Jared was once considered for the role of which superhero?

264. In what murder mystery did Jared appear as Tom in 2005, prior to joining *Supernatural*?

265. Jared was nominated for the Teen Choice award for TV Actor Fantasy/Sci-fi in 2011 and 2012, to whom did he lose out both years?

266. Which other *Supernatural* actor was nominated for the above award, alongside Jared, in 2012?

267. For how many episodes of *Supernatural: The Anime Series* 2011 did Jared voice Sam Winchester?

268. What genre of movie is Jared a fan of?

269. What movie role did Jared audition for in 2010, losing out to Jason Momoa?

270. How many episodes of *Supernatural* Season 6 did Jared direct?

Episode 13 – Unforgiven

271. Who was Sam hunting with in Rhode Island one year previously?

272. To whom do Sam and the above reveal their true identity as hunters?

273. Who do Samuel and Sam use as bait?

274. What happens to the men the female monster has taken?

275. What actor do we see Dean and Sam discussing?

276. How do Dean and Sam get a lead on their next case?

277. How does Dean describe the look the woman in the bar gives Sam?

278. What do the missing women all appear to have in common?

279. Why is Dean concerned about Sam?

280. What are the brothers hunting?

281. How do you kill the above?

282. Who does the monster turn out to be?

283. Why has the above lured Sam back to the town?

284. True or false: Sam feels no guilt about his actions when he was soulless?

285. What happens to Sam at the end of the episode?

Episode 14 – Mannequin 3: The Reckoning

286. What comes to life at the beginning of the episode?

287. What happens to the college janitor?

288. What does Dean give Sam to help him?

289. What murders the security guard at the factory?

290. Who does Dean get a call from requesting his help?

291. Why does the above call really?

292. What does Lisa tell Dean?

293. Who quits their job after the missing girl, Rose Brown, disappears?

294. What does Sam accuse Johnny of being – heartless, nervous or angry?

295. Who is the next potential victim and who saves him?

296. What had the victims done to Rose?

297. How does she die?

298. Who is the next victim of death by dummy?

299. What body part does Isabel (Rose's sister) have of hers?

300. What does Rose possess belonging to Dean?

Season 6 Cast Appearances

301. What Canadian actress plays the role of Gwen Campbell in *Supernatural* Season 6?

302. What role does actor Corin Nemec play in this series?

303. Which one of three fateful sisters does actress Katie Walder play in Season 6?

304. Actor Rick Worthy who plays the alpha vampire in *Supernatural* Season 6 also appeared in the final episode of which TV drama with Jensen Ackles?

305. What monster does Canadian actress Laura Mennell play in *Supernatural* Season 6?

306. Actress Kim Johnston-Ulrich appears as Dr Eleanor Visyak in three episodes of Season 6, can you name them?

307. What actor, who starred as Sam Braddock in *Flashpoint*, plays the role of Mark Campbell in *Supernatural* Season 6

308. What angel does actor Carlos Sanz play in episode 15 'The French Mistake' – Virgil, Raphael or Balthazar?

309. What truthful monster does actress Serinda Swan play in *Supernatural* Season 6?

310. Can you name the actor who plays Gavin Macleod, Crowley's son, in episode 4 'Weekend at Bobby's'?

311. What do actors Roger Haskett, Robert Englund and Kim Johnston-Ulrich have in common in Season 6?

312. Actress Lindsey McKeon returns to *Supernatural* in Season 6, playing what deathly role?

313. Which member of the Campbell family does Brendon
Zub play in *Supernatural* Season 6?

314. What supernatural creature does actor Robert Picardo
play in Season 6?

315. Can you name the two actresses who play Eve,
mother of all monsters, in *Supernatural* Season 6?

Episode 15 – The French Mistake

316. Who does Balthazar say is after Dean and Sam at the beginning of the episode?

317. What does he give to the brothers, before telling them to run?

318. Where do Dean and Sam end up?

319. How do the TV crew refer to Dean and Sam which surprises them?

320. Who do Dean and Sam call?

321. What does the key open?

322. What actor sends out a live Tweet in the same way as his character, during this episode?

323. What does the first Tweet say?

324. What does J Ackles have in his trailer?

325. What soap is on the laptop screen, staring the above?

326. What does Jared have in his backyard?

327. Who is Jared married to in this episode?

328. What happens to Misha Collins?

329. How does Virgil describe his job?

330. Who has the weapons at the end of the episode – Balthazar, Castiel or Raphael?

Episode 16 – …And Then There Were None

331. Who does the truck driver suggest that Eve needs in her life?

332. What does she do to him?

333. When the truck driver goes home what does he do?

334. What does Bobby say has increased?

335. Who is already investigating when Bobby arrives at the scene of the next attack?

336. What do Bobby and the above hunter discover in the victim's ear?

337. What kind of factory do they visit?

338. Who is there already?

339. Who does Dean shoot?

340. What crawls out of Dean's ear?

341. Who is next to be infected with the above – Bobby, Sam or Samuel?

342. Who shoots Samuel?

343. Who stabs Rufus while under the influence of the Khan worm?

344. Who is responsible for creating this new monster?

345. Who has died at the end of the episode and what does Bobby pour on his grave?

Mitch Pileggi (Samuel Campbell)

346. What is Mitch's middle name – Charles, Craig or Colin?

347. In what year was Mitch born in Portland, Oregon?

348. Can you name Mitch's father and mother?

349. What two sports did Mitch excel at during high school?

350. In what country did Mitch spend most of his teenage years?

351. What university did Mitch attend?

352. True or false: Mitch studied Performing Arts at university?

353. Mitch is married to which actress?

354. Mitch has one daughter, can you name her?

355. In what 1992 movie, starring Michael Douglas, did Mitch play an Internal Affairs investigator?

356. What character does Mitch play in *The X-Files*?

357. In which TV series did Mitch play the role of Colonel Steven Caldwell?

358. What medical drama TV series did Mitch appear in 2007-2010?

359. What is the first episode of *Supernatural* in which Mitch's character, Samuel Campbell appears?

360. Up to Season 6, Samuel Campbell dies twice, which two characters kill him?

Episode 17 – My Heart Will Go On

361. How does the man at the beginning of the episode die?

362. What movie series is being parodied in this episode?

363. What car are Dean and Sam driving?

364. Who appears at Bobby's house?

365. What does she say is her relationship to Bobby?

366. What do the victims have in common?

367. What is found at the scene of all the victims?

368. What is the name of the First Mate?

369. Who is the above in reality?

370. Why does the above angel sink the *Titanic*?

371. How does Balthazar describe Celine Dion?

372. Who is killing the survivors of the *Titanic*?

373. Why is the above angry?

374. On whose command does Balthazar sink the *Titanic*?

375. Why does he do this?

Episode 18 – Frontierland

376. Who is the sheriff in the opening sequence?

377. How much later is the next scene?

378. What do Dean, Sam and Bobby discover hidden under Samuel's study?

379. On what date was the phoenix killed?

380. Where do Dean, Sam and Bobby learn about this?

381. True or false: Dean's plan involves time travel?

382. What purchases does Dean come back with?

383. Where does Castiel send Dean and Sam?

384. Who is being hung and why?

385. What cowboy movie star pseudonym does Dean use?

386. Who confronts and attacks Castiel?

387. What can give Castiel his power back?

388. How does Dean kill the phoenix?

389. Back in the present time, who knocks on the door?

390. What's in the box?

Sebastian Roché (Balthazar)

391. In what country was Sebastian born in 1964?

392. What nationality is Sebastian's mother?

393. During his early life, where did Sebastian live for six years – in a gypsy caravan, on a sailboat or with a circus?

394. At what prestigious French academy did Sebastian study drama?

395. How many languages does Sebastian speak?

396. In what 1986 TV film adaptation did Sebastian have an uncredited role as Henri?

397. Can you name Sebastian's actress wife, whom he married in 2014?

398. After *Supernatural*, in 2011, in what supernatural TV drama did Sebastian play Mikael Mikaelson?

399. In what spin-off series of the above, did Sebastian play the same character in 2013?

400. What character did Sebastian play in *General Hospital* between 2007-2015?

401. In what TV series did Sebastian play Thomas Jerome Newton?

402. In what animated movie did Sebastian voice the part of Pedro in 2011?

403. What character did Sebastian play in the 2014 movie *A Walk Among the Tombstones*, starring Liam Neeson?

404. True or false: Sebastian is sometimes mistaken for British chef, Gordon Ramsay?

405. In how many episodes of *Supernatural* Season 6 does Sebastian's character, Balthazar, appear?

Episode 19 – Mommy Dearest

406. How does the mother of all give the people their 'gifts'?

407. Who is Eve hidden from?

408. Who do Dean and Sam ask for help in finding Eve?

409. What power does Eve have over monsters?

410. What happens to Castiel when he visits the town where Eve is?

411. What do Dean and Castiel find hidden on Doctor Bright's porch?

412. What do they find in Marshall's house?

413. What is weird about the monsters Eve is creating?

414. What does Dean name the new species?

415. What is the above name a reference to?

416. What is in the shotguns that they hope will kill Eve?

417. Who does Eve want Dean and Sam to help her to capture?

418. How does Dean kill Eve?

419. True or false: Castiel kills the remaining monsters in the diner?

420. What do Sam and Bobby believe Castiel has done?

Episode 20 – The Man Who Would Be King

421. Who is praying/reminiscing at the beginning of the episode?

422. How does Dean refer to Crowley?

423. What is Sam hunting?

424. Who is torturing monsters?

425. What does Crowley say Castiel smells of?

426. Who do we discover rescued Sam from hell?

427. What does Crowley tell Castiel to do?

428. What is Castiel's heaven?

429. How does Castiel describe freedom?

430. How does Crowley 'improve' hell?

431. True or false: Crowley suggests that Castiel starts a civil war in heaven?

432. What does Castiel say that alerts Dean, Sam and Bobby to the fact that he has been spying on them?

433. How do Dean, Sam and Bobby trap Castiel?

434. How does Crowley suggest that Castiel wins heaven?

435. What does Castiel ask God for at the end of the episode?

All About Meg

436. Can you name the two actresses who have played the role of Meg in *Supernatural*?

437. From whom does Meg take her name?

438. What superpowers and abilities does Meg possess?

439. What kind of vessel does Meg appear to prefer?

440. In *Supernatural* Season 1, who does Meg work for?

441. How does Meg refer to the above?

442. Who is her next boss?

443. Meg trained as a torturer in hell, which white-eyed demon was her mentor?

444. Which hunter does Meg possess in Season 2 – Bobby, Dean or Sam?

445. In what episode of *Supernatural* Season 6 does Meg reappear?

446. What career does Meg say her Season 6 vessel wanted to follow?

447. True or false: Meg kills Crowley in *Supernatural* Season 6?

448. How can Meg be killed?

449. Which member of the Campbell family, while possessed by a demon, tortures Meg in Season 6?

450. What happens to Meg in her last Season 6 appearance?

Episode 21 – Let It Bleed

451. In what year was the beginning sequence set?

452. Can you name the writer who dies at the start of the episode?

453. In what genre does the above write?

454. Which member of the Campbell family's journal is missing?

455. Who is attacked and held prisoner?

456. By whom are they attacked?

457. Who is killed in the attack?

458. How does Crowley refer to Sam?

459. Who do Dean and Sam summon – Castiel, Crowley or Balthazar?

460. What does the 'H' stand for in H.P. Lovecraft?

461. Who is the last survivor of the 1937 dinner party?

462. What does the above say came through the door that was opened?

463. Who decides to join the Winchesters?

464. Who is possessed by a demon?

465. What does Castiel do to Lisa and Ben (requested by Dean)?

Episode 22 – The Man Who Knew Too Much

466. Who is Sam running from at the beginning?

467. What does Sam say is wrong with him?

468. What book is on the pub bookshelf?

469. What does Sam later remember?

470. What famous musicians are on Sam's fake ID?

471. What happens to Eleanor?

472. What do you need to open Purgatory?

473. What does Castiel do to Sam?

474. How does Sam describe Dean?

475. Who is following Sam in his mind?

476. Who is Robin the bartender in reality?

477. True or false: Crowley kills Balthazar?

478. How does Castiel fool Crowley and Rafael?

479. What does Castiel do to Rafael?

480. How does the episode end?

481. In what year was Fergus Roderick MacLeod born?

482. The Impala is the namesake of what kind of animal?

483. Who makes an unexpected guest appearance as himself in episode 15 'The French Mistake'?

484. Who directed the above episode?

485. Episode 1 'Exile on Main St.' shares its title with an album by British rock group The Rolling Stones, can you name two episodes in previous seasons that were also named after a song or album by the band?

486. Can you name another Season 6 episode named after an album by the Rolling Stones?

487. Which actor was particularly keen to shoot episode 18 'Frontierland' having a lifelong love of westerns?

488. In episode 4 'Weekend at Bobby's' which actor's voice is heard reading the news on Bobby's TV?

489. Which writer and producer joined *Supernatural* in Season 6, episode 2 'Two and a Half Men' being the first he wrote for the series?

490. Kevin Parks, one of the first assistant directors on *Supernatural* Season 6, is known for his knowledge of what?

491. Brett Matthews joined the *Supernatural* team for Season 6, in what capacity?

492. Which episode of *Supernatural* Season 6 contains several references to the *Twilight* series, including the title?

493. In episode 21 'Let It Bleed' what comic series is Ben
reading?

494. The above is based on a mythical universe created by
which horror writer?

495. Who is Andrew Dabb's writing partner on
Supernatural Season 6?

496. What episode of Season 6 did *Supernatural* writer
Ben Edlund direct?

497. Can you name Eric Charmelo's main writing partner
on *Supernatural*, both joining the team for Season 6?

498. Episode 17 'My Heart Will Go On' is the title song
by Celine Dion from *Titanic* (1997), what Season 4
episode also makes reference to the multi-award
winning movie?

499. Episode 22 'The Man Who Knew Too Much' was
written and directed by two key members of the
Supernatural production team, can you name them?

500. Which long-term *Supernatural* writer and producer
took over as show-runner for Season 6?

'Ever since I came back, I am… a better hunter than
I've ever been! Nothing scares me anymore!'

~ Sam Winchester

Answers

Episode 1 – Exile on Main St.

1. Holy water and a gun

2. Pest control

3. A devil's trap

4. Claw marks (on the lamp post, wall and garage door), blood and sulphur

5. Azazel

6. He has been poisoned, Sam

7. Cuts himself with a silver blade, drinks holy water and salt

8. Nearly a year; their resurrected grandfather, Samuel Campbell, and cousins; Gwen, Christian, Mark and Johnny Campbell

9. Bobby's house

10. So that he could live a normal life, away from hunting

11. Djinn, for revenge

12. Johnny

13. Capture her and take her away (unbeknown to Dean)

14. False: He remains with Lisa and Ben in order to protect them

15. The Impala

Episode 2 – Two and a Half Men

16. Babies

17. For being interested in a gun from his car

18. They all have home security from the same company
     (Harper Caine)

19. A baby

20. How to use a gun

21. A shapeshifter

22. Alcohol

23. That it is the baby of a shapeshifter

24. The baby's shapeshifter father is killed by Dean

25. The Campbells' hideout

26. Samuel Campbell

27. Bullets and knives have no effect on it

28. It is an alpha shapeshifter

29. Mark

30. That Dean should return to hunting and visit when he
     could

Season 6 Episode Titles

31. The Third Man (episode 3)

32. Like a Virgin (episode 12)

33. The Man Who Would Be King (episode 20)

34. Mommie Dearest (episode 19)

35. Two and a Half Men (episode 2)

36. Clap Your Hands If You Believe (episode 9) – 'Do you believe in fairies? …If you believe clap your hands.'

37. Caged Heat (episode 10)

38. And Then There Were None (episode 16)

39. You Can't Handle the Truth (episode 6)

40. The French Mistake (episode 15)

41. Frontierland (episode 18)

42. All Dogs Go To Heaven (episode 8)

43. My Heart Will Go On (episode 17)

44. The Man Who Knew Too Much (episode 22)

45. Family Matters (episode 7)

Episode 3 – The Third Man

46. Lisa Braeden

47. Lying

48. The boy has no face

49. Castiel

50. A more profound bond

51. The Staff of Moses

52. His 'people skills'

53. Aaron Birch

54. False: He exchanged his soul with an angel

55. Balthazar

56. Cut into pieces

57. He performs a painful reading on Aaron that involves reaching inside his chest

58. Raphael

59. Turns him into a pillar of salt (using Lot's salt)

60. That since he has been resurrected, he feels different

Episode 4 – Weekend at Bobby's

61. Jensen Ackles

62. The return of his soul/to be released from his deal with Crowley

63. That he is the King of Hell

64. Lucky the Leprechaun

65. Ginger peach cobbler

66. Fergus MacLeod

67. Rufus Turner

68. Marcy

69. By putting her in Marcy's wood chipper

70. He swallows it

71. Two of 'the whiniest, most self-absorbed sons of bitches' he has ever met

72. For 'An extra three inches below the belt'

73. Sheriff Jody Mills

74. Dean and Sam – to dig up (ready to burn) the mortal remains of Fergus MacLeod

75. True

Season 6 Quotes

76. Meg (episode 10 'Caged Heat')

77. Death (episode 11 'Appointment in Samarra')

78. Lisa Braeden (episode 1 'Exile on Main St.')

79. Crowley (episode 20 'The Man Who Would Be King')

80. Sam Winchester (episode 8 'All Dogs Go To Heaven')

81. Balthazar (episode 3 'The Third Man')

82. Bobby Singer (referring to demons, episode 4, 'Weekend at Bobby's')

83. Rufus (to Bobby, episode 16 'And Then There Were None')

84. Castiel (to Dean, episode 7 'Family Matters')

85. Alpha vampire (episode 6 'Family Matters')

86. Crowley (to Bobby, episode 4 'Weekend at Bobby's')

87. Dean Winchester (episode 19 'Mommy Dearest')

88. Eve (episode 16 'And Then There Were None')

89. Crowley (episode 21 'Let It Bleed')

90. Samuel Colt (episode 18 'Frontierland')

Episode 5 – Live Free or Twihard

91. The Black Rose

92. Kristen

93. Pattinson

94. *The Twilight Saga*

95. Robert

96. Seven

97. Vampire

98. He is turned into a vampire

99. Sam

100. Lisa Braeden

101. Samuel Campbell (his journal)

102. Drink a human's blood, 'feed'

103. A fang from the vampire that infected him

104. The vampires' 'father' or the alpha

105. Build an army

Episode 6 – You Can't Handle the Truth

106. Kill her/burn her alive in her sleep

107. That he is 'his case'

108. She tucked her hair behind her ear

109. He drills him to death

110. They were both having music lessons at the same music store

111. Gabriel's Horn of Truth

112. Veritas, the God of Truth

113. They vanish from the morgue

114. He says, "I would just like to know the fricking truth"

115. That he gets a pedicure once a month and Dean is his favourite

116. Unhealthy

117. Ashley Frank, a reporter and host of *Frank Talk*

118. Lie to her

119. That since returning from Lucifer's cage, he has been unable to feel anything

120. True

Season 6 Soundtrack

Episode 7 – Family Matters

136. He can no longer sleep

137. That Sam has no soul

138. As tall as the Chrysler building

139. Samuel Campbell

140. Yes, his soul is intact

141. Taking them captive 'grilling' them, not killing them

142. Dead man's blood

143. Torture him by driving nails in his hands and feet and electrocuting him

144. The first vampire

145. Purgatory

146. A demon

147. Crowley, the King of Hell

148. True

149. *Charlie's Angels*

150. Sam's soul

Episode 8 – All Dogs Go To Heaven

151. He is attacked by an unseen creature in his car

152. Crowley

153. Burn his hand

154. If Dean and Sam catch an alpha, he'll give Sam his soul back

155. Because it is not a full moon

156. That werewolves have been acting strangely for some time

157. His chest is ripped open and his heart is missing (second case in two days)

158. His brother and landlord

159. He is attacked by his girlfriend's dog, Lucky

160. It turns into a human

161. Mandy, Cal's girlfriend

162. Lucky transforming into a human man

163. He gets hit by a car, whilst running away from Sam

164. Skin walker – can change anywhere, anytime, can infect with a single bite

165. That Dean was right, he is not the same Sam, he doesn't care about people or about Dean

Season 6 Monsters

166. Djinn are tattooed, with unusual glowing eyes

167. Three

168. An alpha shapeshifter is stronger, has a resistance to silver, a higher pain threshold, does not shed skin, and has a bond with its offspring meaning they can locate them.

169. Iridium

170. The very first vampire and the progenitor of all other vampires

171. Roman Goddess of Truth

172. Forcing humans to tell the truth

173. Silver bullet

174. People who have been to their realm or only if they choose to be seen

175. Fairies must count every single grain in front of them

176. With a silver knife blessed by priest/or rosemary and salt heated to a high temperature

177. Large shark

178. A dragon

179. Turn humans into arachne

180. A Khan worm

Episode 9 – Clap Your Hands If You Believe…

181. In a cornfield

182. *The X-Files*

183. UFOs/aliens

184. Fairies

185. His conscience

186. Patrick

187. In bed with hippie Sparrow Jennings

188. Sparrow is one of the few women who survive a romantic encounter with Sam up to this point

189. Puts 'her' in the microwave

190. First born sons

191. Leave a bowl of cream, iron, silver and by spilling sugar and salt (they have to count each grain)

192. To save his watchmaking business

193. Because he tackles a little man thinking it was the man in the hat who had been following him

194. It 'hits them like tequila'

195. By spilling salt (the leprechaun then has to count the grains) and reading a ritual to banish the fairies

Episode 10 – Caged Heat

196. Himself

197. Alpha shapeshifter

198. Iridium

199. Meg, the demon

200. That she works with Dean and Sam

201. *Raiders of the Lost Ark*

202. Porn

203. It has been locked in the cage with Lucifer and Michael for over a year and may have been subjected to torture

204. He has promised to bring Samuel's daughter, Mary, (Dean and Sam's mother) back to life

205. Hellhounds

206. By using an angel banishing sigil

207. True

208. Ghouls

209. In a devil's trap

210. Burns his bones and kills him

Jensen Ackles (Dean Winchester)

211. Justin

212. Justin sounded too ordinary so they changed his name to Jensen

213. Pisces (born 1 March 1978)

214. 6 foot 1 inch

215. Daneel Harris

216. True

217. *Batman Under the Red Hood*

218. Batman

219. Demonic forces: Marlena, his character's mother was possessed by the devil in *Days of Our Lives*, Jensen played the son of Satan in *Devour* and the Winchester brothers hunt demons in *Supernatural*.

220. Yes

221. Best actor

222. All Hell Breaks Loose: parts I and II

223. Gibson

224. Sam Winchester

225. Episode 4 'Weekend at Bobby's'

Episode 11 – Appointment in Samarra

226. Dr Robert

227. Above a Chinese grocer

228. Three

229. Death

230. Get his soul back and put up a wall from his time in hell

231. Dean has to be Death for a day (and must keep Death's ring on)

232. Tessa

233. Balthazar

234. Bobby

235. He has a trap door that Sam falls down

236. A drink driver was about to crash his car into a bus

237. Hilary, a 12-year-old girl

238. Death

239. A burger

240. True

Episode 12 – Like a Virgin

241. A dragon

242. It has been skinned alive

243. The field, Lucifer and falling

244. Her diary

245. They are all virgins

246. World of Warcraft

247. Doctor Visyak

248. Sword of Brunswick

249. Dynamite

250. False: It was Castiel, not Bobby, who reveals the truth

251. Sewers

252. Gold

253. Human skin

254. To use as a vessel (for Mother)

255. Mother of All

Jared Padalecki (Sam Winchester)

256. *Silent Witness*

257. *Gilmore Girls*

258. Cancer (born 19 July 1982)

259. 6 foot 4 inches

260. Genevieve Cortese (Ruby, Season 4)

261. Sun Valley, Idaho

262. False: Jared is extremely superstitious

263. Clarke Kent/Superman

264. *Cry Wolf*

265. Ian Somerhalder for *The Vampire Diaries*

266. Jensen Ackles

267. 22 episodes

268. Horror

269. *Conan the Barbarian* (2011)

270. None of them

Episode 13 – Unforgiven

271. His grandfather, Samuel Campbell

272. Sheriff Roy Dobbs and his wife, Brenna

273. Sheriff Roy Dobbs

274. They are poisoned and bound in a web/they are later shot by Sam

275. Bill Gibson

276. An unknown number texts them coordinates

277. "She just cougar-eyed you"

278. They all slept with Sam when he was in town one year ago

279. His memory of the hunt is returning and he might therefore start to recall his time in Lucifer's cage

280. An arachne

281. Chop of their heads

282. Roy Dobbs

283. For revenge

284. False: Sam feels responsible for his actions and guilty of the way he behaved

285. Sam has convulsions as he remembers his time in hell

Episode 14 – Mannequin 3: The Reckoning

286. Anatomical dummy

287. He is killed by the above

288. Joe, grub and effective medication

289. A mannequin

290. Ben Braeden

291. A 'parent trap' for Lisa and Dean (to get them back together)

292. That she is trying to get over him

293. The janitor killed by the dummy

294. Nervous

295. Johnny, he is saved by Sam

296. Made her think she had a secret admirer

297. She trips, falls and hits her head/they bury her in the woods

298. Johnny

299. Her kidney

300. The Impala

Season 6 Cast Appearances

301. Jessica Heafey

302. Christian Campbell

303. Atropos, one of the three Fates

304. *Dark Angel*

305. Djinn, Brigitta

306. Episode 12 'Like a Virgin', episode 21 'Let It Bleed' and episode 22 'The Man Who Knew Too Much'

307. David Paetkau

308. Virgil

309. Veritas, Goddess of Truth

310. Adam Groves

311. They all play a type of doctor: Dr Paul Connelly (dentist), Dr Robert and Dr Eleanor Visyak

312. Tessa, the reaper

313. Johnny

314. Leprachaun

315. Julia Maxwell and Samantha Smith

Episode 15 – The French Mistake

316. Raphael

317. A key

318. On the set of *Supernatural*

319. Jensen and Jared

320. Castiel

321. A room where Balthazar has hidden all the weapons he stole from heaven

322. Misha Collins (Castiel)

323. 'Hola Mishamigos, J2 got me good. Really starting to feel like one of the guys'

324. An aquarium and a model helicopter

325. *Days of our Lives*

326. An alpaca

327. Genevieve Padalecki (Ruby) as in real life

328. He is stabbed to death

329. He is the weapons keeper of heaven

330. Castiel

Episode 16 – ...And Then There Were None

73

331. Jesus
332. Whispers/puts something in his ear
333. Kills his wife and family (with a hammer)
334. Incidences of ghouls, vampires, werewolves
335. Rufus
336. Black goo
337. Canning factory
338. Samuel and Gwen Campbell
339. Gwen
340. A (Khan) worm
341. Samuel
342. Sam
343. Bobby
344. Eve
345. Rufus, Johnny Walker Blue Label whisky

Mitch Pileggi (Samuel Campbell)

346. Craig

347. 1952

348. Vito and Maxine

349. Football and wrestling

350. Turkey

351. University of Texas at Austin

352. False: He studied Business

353. Arlene Warren

354. Sawyer Scout Pileggi

355. *Basic Instinct*

356. Walter Skinner

357. *Stargate: Atlantis*

358. *Grey's Anatomy*

359. Season 4, episode 3 'In the Beginning'

360. Azazel (Season 4), Sam Winchester (Season 6)

Episode 17 – My Heart Will Go On

361. He slips on a ping pong ball and falls under the garage door

362. *Final Destination*

363. Mustang with orange stripes

364. Ellen (Harvelle)

365. Wife

366. They came to America on the same boat in the same year (*Titanic* 1912)

367. Gold thread

368. I.P. Freely

369. Balthazar

370. He doesn't like the movie (*Titanic*) or the soundtrack by Celine Dion 'My Heart Will Go On'

371. As a destitute lounge singer

372. One of the Fates (Atropos)

373. Dean and Sam averted the Apocalypse meaning Fate no longer has a role and everything is in chaos

374. Castiel's

375. So that he would have 50,000 more souls

Episode 18 – Frontierland

Sebastian Roché (Balthazar)

391. France (Paris)

392. British (Scottish)

393. On a sailboat

394. Conservatoire National Supérieur d'art Dramatique (CNSAD)

395. Four: English, French, Italian and Spanish

396. *The Murders in the Rue Morgue*

397. Alicia Hannah

398. *The Vampire Diaries*

399. *The Originals*

400. Jerry Jacks/James Craig

401. *Fringe*

402. *The Adventures of Tintin: The Secret of the Unicorn*

403. Yuri Landau

404. True

405. Six: Episode 3 'The Third Man', episode 11 'Appointment in Samarra', episode 15 'The French Mistake', episode 17 ' My Heart Will Go On', episode 21 'Let It Bleed' and episode 22 'The Man Who Knew Too Much'

Episode 19 – Mommy Dearest

406. Touches them/kisses them

407. All angels

408. Lenore (vampire)

409. Psychic connection

410. He becomes powerless

411. Ed's dead body

412. A room full of dead bodies that all look like Ed

413. They are hybrids (ie the girl in the bar is half vampire, half wraith)

414. Jefferson Starships

415. They are a band with a long history

416. Phoenix ash

417. Crowley

418. He takes phoenix ash with his whiskey, then Eve bites him

419. True: He gets his powers back when Eve dies

420. Faked Crowley's death

Episode 20 – The Man Who Would Be King

421. Castiel

422. Satan Junior

423. Djinn

424. Crowley

425. The Impala

426. Castiel

427. Kill the Winchesters

428. The eternal Tuesday afternoon of an autistic man who drowned in the bathtub in 1953

429. A length of rope that God wants you to hang yourself with

430. By making everyone who comes down wait in line

431. True

432. Superman going to the dark side/kryptonite

433. In a burning ring of holy oil

434. By opening the door to Purgatory and taking souls

435. A sign

All About Meg

436. Nicki Aycox and Rachel Minor

437. Meg Masters, her first vessel

438. Superhuman strength, telepathy, telekinesis and the ability to teleport. She can also possess humans and inflict pain on other demons and humans.

439. Attractive young women

440. Azazel

441. Father

442. Lucifer

443. Alastair

444. Sam

445. Episode 10 'Caged Heat'

446. Acting

447. False: Meg is overpowered by Crowley and Castiel kills him by burning his mortal remains

448. With Ruby's knife, an angel blade or the Colt

449. Christian

450. She escapes and disappears

Episode 21 – Let It Bleed

451. 1937 (15 March)

452. H.P. Lovecraft

453. Horror

454. Moishe

455. Lisa and Ben

456. Crowley

457. Matt, Lisa's new boyfriend

458. Jolly Green (as in Jolly Green Giant)

459. Balthazar

460. Howard (Phillips)

461. The maid's son

462. A monster from Purgatory that went into his mother, Eleanor (Ellie)

463. Balthazar

464. Lisa

465. Wipes their memories so that they forget about Dean

Episode 22 – The Man Who Knew Too Much

466. The police

467. He has amnesia and has forgotten who he is

468. One written by H.P. Lovecraft

469. The name of a hotel; the Nite Owl

470. Jimmy Page, Neil Peart and Angus Young

471. She is tortured by Castiel and Crowley

472. Blood of a virgin, blood from a native of Purgatory and eclipse of a full moon

473. He takes down the wall

474. A 'male model type'

475. He is (Sam)

476. A girl Sam killed when he was soulless

477. False: Balthazar is killed by Castiel

478. By swapping the blood

479. Makes him explode

480. Castiel declares that he is the new God, 'a better one' and Dean and Sam have to bow down and profess their devotion

481. 1661 (Crowley)

482. Antelope

483. Eric Kripke

484. Charles Beeson

485. 'Time is on My Side' (Season 3, episode 15) and 'Sympathy for the Devil' (Season 5, episode 1)

486. Episode 21 'Let It Bleed'

487. Jensen Ackles

488. Alan Ackles (Jensen's father)

489. Adam Glass

490. He is known for his encyclopedic knowledge of the show, earning him the nickname 'Parksapedia'

491. Writer and executive story editor

492. Episode 5 'Live Free or Twihard' (Twihard is the name of an obsessive fan of *Twilight*)

493. *Cthulhu Tales*

494. H.P. Lovecraft (Cthulhu Mythos)

495. Daniel Loflin

496. Episode 20 'The Man Who Would Be King'

497. Nicole Snyder

498. 'Heaven and Hell' (Dean and Anna have sex in the back of the Impala, referencing a scene in *Titanic*)

499. Written by Eric Kripke and directed by Robert Singer

500. Sera Gamble

Also by

Light Bulb Quizzes

The Supernatural Quiz Book

Seasons 1, 2, 3, 4 and 5.

Follow Light Bulb Quizzes

on

Twitter: @LightBulbQuiz

and

Facebook.com/Lightbulbquizzes

For news, giveaways
and forthcoming projects